THE
Christmas
Boot

by Lisa Wheeler

Illustrations by Michael Glenn Monroe

Merry Christmas!

Michael Monroe

mitten press

For my dear friend, Theresa Griffin, who believed in me
long before I believed in myself.
–L.W.

All inquiries should be addressed to:
Mitten Press
An imprint of Ann Arbor Media Group LLC
2500 S. State Street
Ann Arbor, MI 48104

Printed and bound in China.

10   9   8   7   6   5   4   3   2   1

Library of Congress Cataloging-in-Publication Data

Wheeler, Lisa, 1963-
The Christmas boot / by Lisa Wheeler ; illustrated by Michael Glenn Monroe.
p. cm.
Summary: When lonely old Miss Hannah Greyweather finds a boot
in the woods, it fills her life with warmth and magic, but she knows even
before its true owner appears that she will have to return it.
ISBN-13: 978-1-58726-327-9 (hardcover)
ISBN-10: 1-58726-327-0 (hardcover)
[1. Boots--Fiction. 2. Magic--Fiction. 3. Lost and found possessions--Fiction.
4. Santa Claus--Fiction. 5. Christmas--Fiction.] I. Monroe, Michael Glenn, ill. II. Title.
PZ7.W5657Chr 2007
[E]--dc22
2006035744

Book and jacket design by Somberg Design
www.sombergdesign.com

Deep in the forest on Christmas morning, Miss Hannah Greyweather gathered bundles of kindling wood. For her, this day was no different than any other. As she went about her daily chores, she chatted to the forest, she talked to the mountains, but mostly she spoke to herself.

"Brrrrr," she said to the mountain. "Will this cold winter ever be over? It chills my bones."

The mountain didn't answer.

Her arms were nearly full when, just past the spruce grove, near the edge of the clearing, she spotted something. In the snow, deepest black upon purest white, lay a boot.

"Glory be!" Hannah exclaimed to the forest. "Who could've lost this?" The forest remained silent.

And since her arms were so full of twigs, and since her feet were fully freezing, and since it looked to be such a nice boot, she slipped her rag-wrapped right foot deep within it.

"Ahhh," Hannah said. "That does feel nice."

It surely must, for when she slid her tiny foot into the very large boot, it suddenly took on the shape and size of Hannah's own foot. It fit perfectly.

Hannah headed back to her ramshackle cabin, limping her way through the snow. Her warm right foot stepped surely as her cold left foot struggled to keep up.

"This boot was quite a find," Hannah said to the walls of her cabin. "Where do you suppose it came from?"

The walls did not reply.

As she slipped into bed that night, she stared at the boot on the floor and said, "I only wish I had your mate." Then, Hannah drifted off to sleep.

In the morning, Hannah arose to begin her daily chores.

"Come on, boot," she said. "Time to get to work." But as she focused her eyes, she didn't see one black boot. She saw two black boots!

"Glory be!" Hannah said to the left boot. "How did you get in here?"

The boot couldn't say.

Then Hannah Greyweather placed both her tiny feet into those warm black boots. They fit most comfortably.

As she went about her wood gathering, Hannah had a spring in her step that hadn't been there for years. She danced in the spruce grove, skipped along the frozen creek bed, and made snow angels on the hillside. Her feet felt wonderfully warm.

That night, Hannah placed her boots next to her bed and wondered at her good fortune.

"Such a glorious find," she said to the right boot. "Who could have lost such a treasure as you?"

The boot stood silent.

"No matter," said Hannah. "I've made good use of you here. If I had mittens as toasty warm as you, I would surely be the happiest woman in the world."

In the morning, tucked neatly inside of each boot was a bright red mitten.
"Glory be!" Hannah said to the boots. "What form of magic is this?"
The boots couldn't tell.
She placed the mittens on her hands and, like the boots, they were
comfy warm.
"If the boot is magic," Hannah said to the mittens, "will it give me more?
Will it give me a fluffy feather bed? A fabulous feast? A big fancy house?"
The mittens stayed mute.
"I suppose that is too much to ask," said Hannah. "I best get about
my chores."

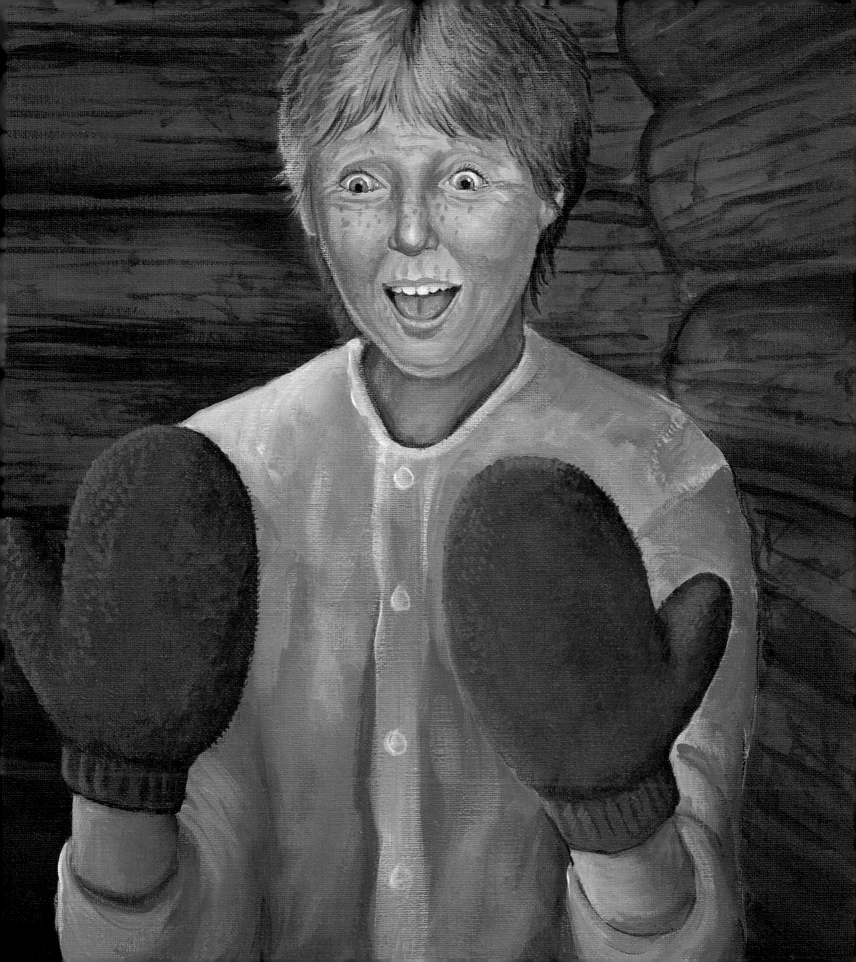

In the woods that day, her feet and hands felt equally
fine. She climbed the mountain trail, gathered chestnuts,
and built a towering snowman.

As she strolled down the path to home, an amazing sight met Hannah's eyes.
A big fancy house had replaced her ramshackle cabin. Luscious smells drifted
from the open doorway, inviting her inside.

"Glory be!" Hannah said to the house. "How did you get here?"

The house couldn't say.

Inside, Hannah wandered from room to room, taking in the loveliness of it all. She tasted the rich foods, she snuggled in the fluffy feather bed. Somehow, it didn't seem fully real. It didn't seem fully right, either. Unlike the wonderful boots and the toasty mittens, the house didn't seem to "fit" Hannah.

Suddenly, there came a KNOCK-KNOCK-KNOCK on the fine front door.

"Who could it be?" Hannah asked the walls. "I've never had company."

She opened the door slowly, cautiously, peeking through the small crack between the door and the wall. What she could see was a round man with a white beard. He wore a red vest, a green tie . . . and one black boot.

"May I help you?" Hannah asked the man.

"Yes," the man answered. "I think you may have found something of mine."

Hannah, happily surprised to hear the sound of another voice, opened the door at once.

"Glory be!" she said. "Come in. Come in. You must be freezing out there."

"Just my right foot," said the round man, with a twinkle in his eye.

Hannah looked down at her own booted feet. "Yes," she said. "I do believe I have something that belongs to you."

She fixed the man a cup of her own herbal tea. She served him the roasted chestnuts she had gathered. They talked of everything, and nothing, deep into the night.

"Now," she said. "I best give you your boot, so you can be on your way."

When the man in red placed his large foot into the boot, it took on the shape and size of his very own foot.

"Ahhh," he said. "That does feel nice."

At once, the big fancy house, the tremendous feast, and the feather bed disappeared. The herbal tea and the roasted chestnuts were all the feast that remained. Even her left boot and red mittens were gone.

"I am sorry," said the man.

"No need," said Hannah. "It is as it should be. The boot didn't belong to me, but I enjoyed it while it was here."

"Is there anything I can give to you?" asked the man. "What do you truly desire?"

"What I truly desire is someone to talk to," said Hannah. "But warm boots and a pair of mittens would be mighty fine."

The man in red winked his eye. Suddenly, there appeared a fine pair of new boots and bright green mittens.

"Thank you, sir," Hannah said, as she walked him to the door and bid him good-bye. "I will make good use of them."

That night, Hannah climbed into bed. "Good-night," she said to her fine new mittens and boots.

"Arf!" the right boot answered.

"What!?" Hannah said, eyeing the boot. She peeked inside. Two black eyes peered back at her.

"Arf! Arf!" she heard again. Then she reached into the boot and pulled a wiggly puppy into her arms.

"Thank you," Hannah whispered to the night sky, as she held her new friend close.

The night sky answered, "Merry Christmas, Hannah! Merry Christmas!"